Luna Loves ART

Joseph Coelho

Fiona Lumbers

Andersen Press

Luna Loves Art.

Today she is going on a school trip.

School trip backpack – check!
School trip lunch box – check!
School trip instant camera – click!

Andy Warhol
Flowers, 1964

Henri Matisse
Blue Nude II, 1952

Pierre Bonnard
Woman at a
Table,
1923

Henry Moore
Family Group, 1949

Andy Warhol
Campbell's
Soup Can, 1962

Acknowledgments

Damien Hirst, Untitled 2 (Spot Painting), 1992 © Damien Hirst and Science Ltd. All rights reserved, DACS 2019.

Andy Warhol, Flowers, 1964 © 2019 The Andy Warhol Foundation for the Visual Arts, Inc./Licensed by DACS, London.

Andy Warhol, Campbell's Soup Can, 1962 © 2019 The Andy Warhol Foundation for the Visual Arts, Inc./Licensed by DACS, London.

Louise Bourgeois, Maman, late 1990s © The Easton Foundation/VAGA at ARS, NY and DACS, London 2019.

Louise Bourgeois, Untitled (Suspended Sculpture), 2004 © The Easton Foundation/VAGA at ARS, NY and DACS, London 2019.

Henri Matisse, Blue Nude II, 1952 © Succession H. Matisse/DACS 2019.

Henri Matisse The Snail, 1953 © Succession H. Matisse/DACS 2019.

Henry Moore, Family Group, 1949 © The Henry Moore Foundation. All Rights Reserved, DACS/www.henry-moore.org
Reproduced by permission of The Henry Moore Foundation

Jackson Pollock © The Pollock-Krasner Foundation ARS, NY and DACS, London 2019.

Pumpkin (Red), Pumpkin (Yellow) 2016 © Yayoi Kusama.

Jeff Koons, Balloon Dog, 1994-2000 Used with permission from the artist.

For all you little artists out there who have found joy in art,
be it in the looking at, immersion in or creation of
this wonderful expression that is for us all. – J.C.

For Sonny & Teddy.
And special thanks to Beccy & Sue. – F.L.

This paperback edition first published in 2021 by Andersen Press Ltd.
First published in Great Britain in 2020 by Andersen Press Ltd.
20 Vauxhall Bridge Road, London SW1V 2SA.
Text copyright © Joseph Coelho 2020.
Illustration copyright © Fiona Lumbers 2020.
The rights of Joseph Coelho and Fiona Lumbers
to be identified as the author and illustrator of
this work have been asserted by them in accordance
with the Copyright, Designs and Patents Act, 1988.
All rights reserved. Printed and bound in China.
10 9 8 7 6 5 4 3 2 1
ISBN 978 1 78344 865 4
British Library Cataloguing in Publication Data available.

Dad drops Luna off at the school gates.
Miss Rosa is waiting with the register.
Luna's mum is a parent helper!

Finn is alone.

Today the class is going to The Art Gallery.

The whole class is excited.
The gallery is the biggest building
Luna has ever seen.

But Finn doesn't care. Finn is looking down.

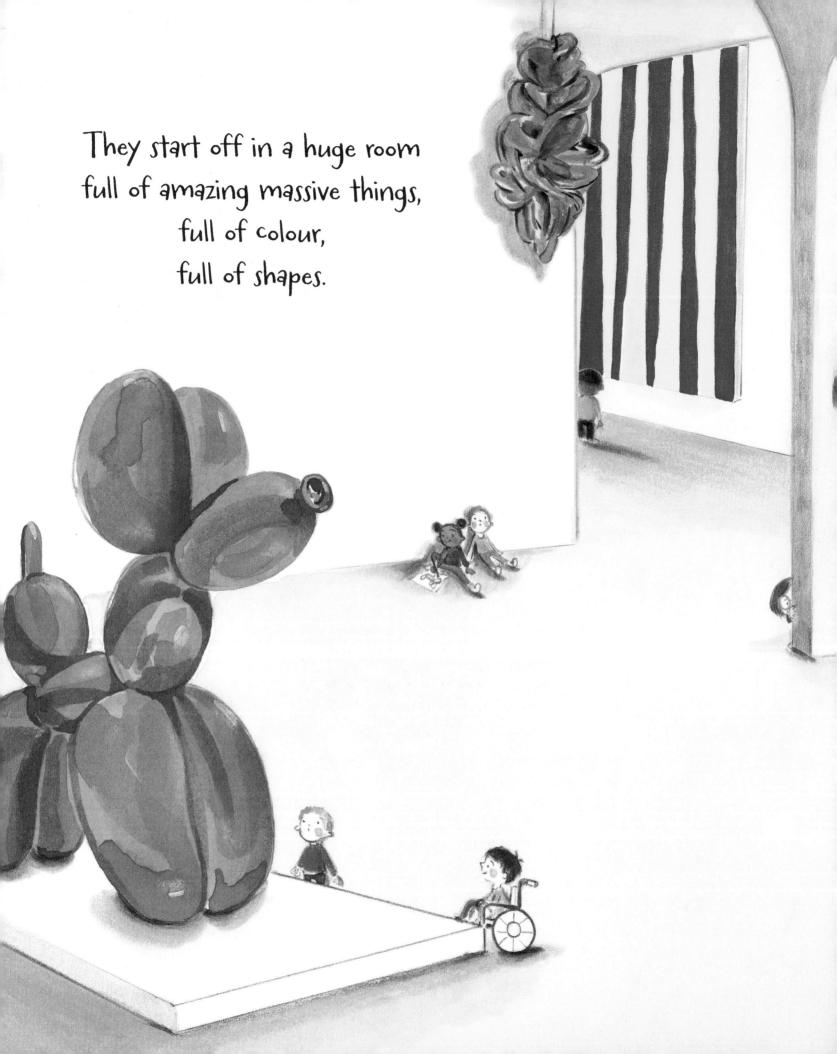

They start off in a huge room
full of amazing massive things,
full of colour,
full of shapes.

"Look at all the art!" says Luna.
Finn is looking up.

Miss Rosa takes the class to
The Impressionist and
Post-Impressionist Rooms.

Vincent Van Gogh's 'Sunflowers' has paint so thick that the flowers look alive.

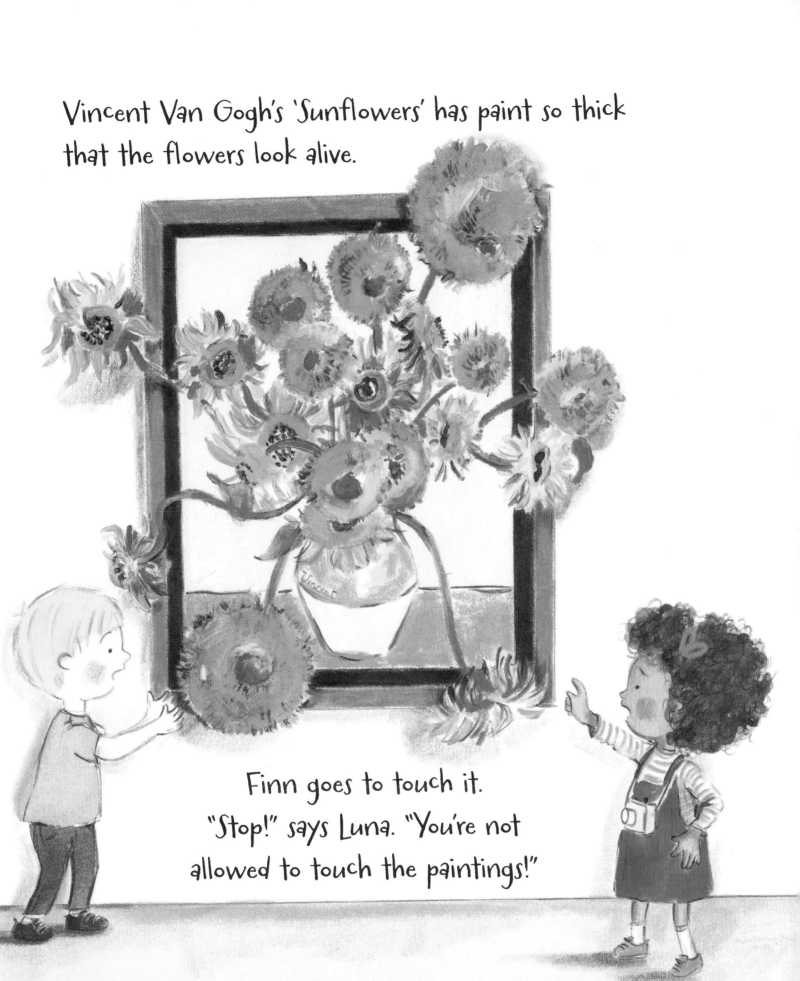

Finn goes to touch it.
"Stop!" says Luna. "You're not allowed to touch the paintings!"

Miss Rosa hands
out some clipboards,
paper and pencils.
Luna does a sketch...
Scribble!

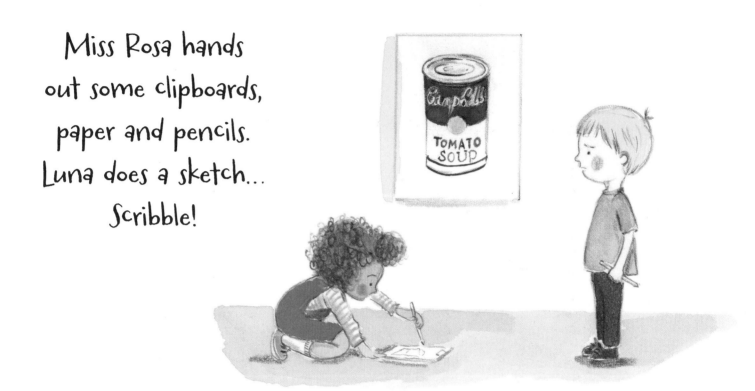

Finn scrunches up
Luna's picture!
"Hey!" says Luna.

Miss Rosa takes
Finn aside.

"Why is he so mean?"
says Luna.
"Maybe he needs a
friend," says Mum.

Miss Rosa takes the class to The Abstract Paintings Room.

Kazimir Malevich's 'Black Square'
is all edged, black and cracked.
A night-time robbed of stars,
A phone waiting to ring.

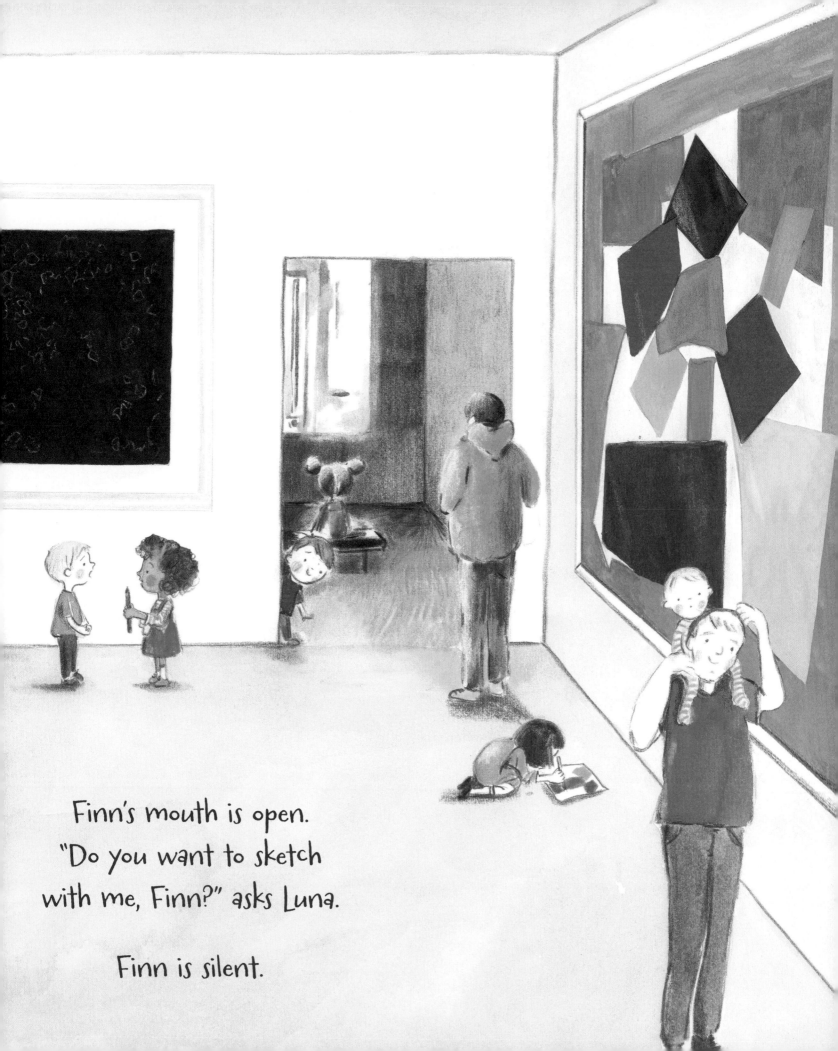

Finn's mouth is open.
"Do you want to sketch
with me, Finn?" asks Luna.

Finn is silent.

Miss Rosa asks the class, "Describe what is happening in Henri Rousseau's 'Surprised!'" "There's a scaredy-cat tiger in the jungle," laughs Luna.

Finn roars at the painting...
"The wind is thrashing, the clouds are dark.
The tiger is angry,
but inside he is cold and wet.
He wanders the jungle
staying in different places all the time.
The tiger is scared and alone
and needs a home."

Mum leads Finn to a quiet corner.
Luna follows.
Henry Moore's 'Family Group'
is big and bronze.
Luna takes a photo... Click!
"Families don't look like that," says Finn.

Mum says...
"Some families look like that, some do not.
Some families are related, some are not.
Some families are together, some are apart,
there are lots of different families like all this different art."

Miss Rosa takes the class to a dark room,
full of lights and sounds.
"We can touch the art!" beams Luna.
"It's incredible," shouts Finn.

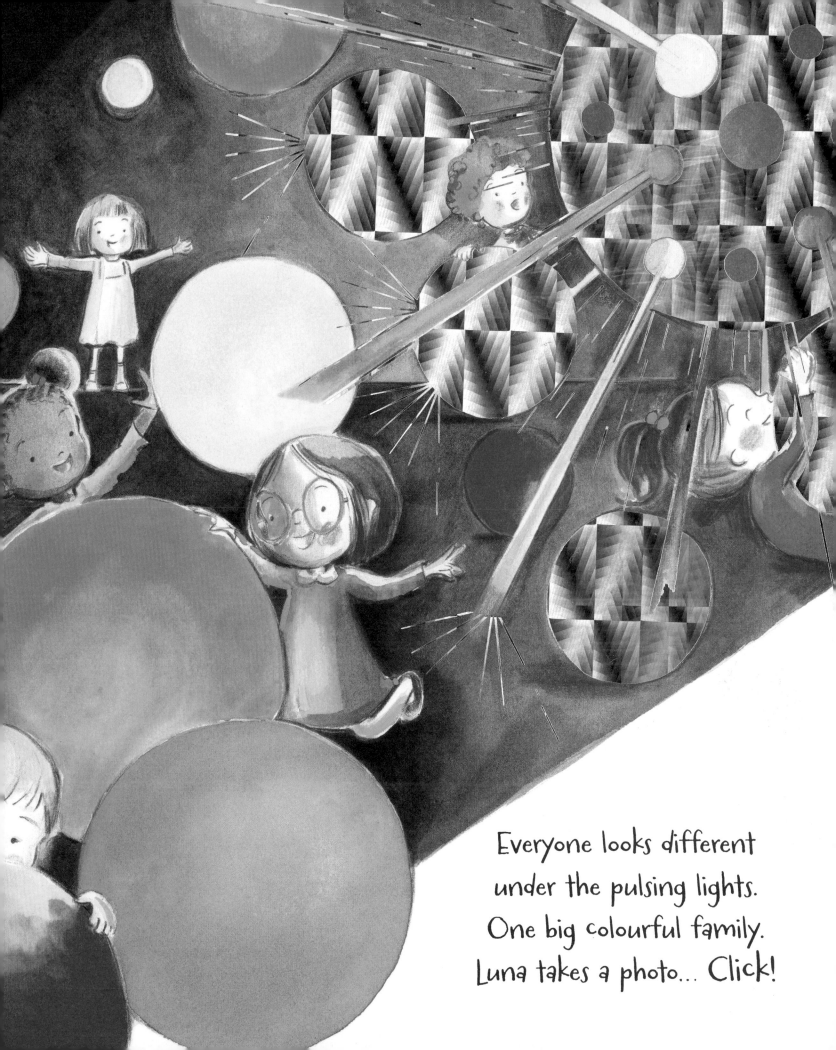

Everyone looks different
under the pulsing lights.
One big colourful family.
Luna takes a photo... Click!

Miss Rosa takes the class to The Art Gallery Shop.
There are erasers, pencils and badges.
Henry Moore keyrings, posters of sunflowers and
black squares, postcards of tigers.
Toys that light up and flash.

Luna gives Finn a photo.
Finn gives Luna a drawing.

Luna and Finn laugh
on the bus back to school,
take photos of the sights
and talk about the art they remember.

Luna and Finn love school trips.
Luna and Finn love Art.

Jackson Pollock

Piet Mondrian Composition II in Red, Blue, and Yellow, 1930

Edouard Manet
Girl with summer hat,
Jeanne Demarsy, 1879

Paul Cezanne
Still Life, Pears
and Green
Apples, 1873

Kazimir Malevich Black Square, 1915

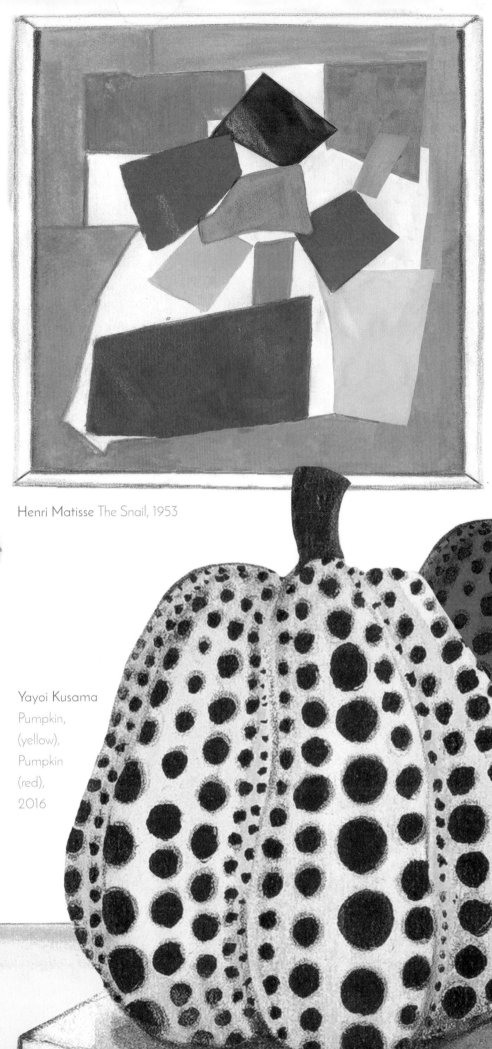

Henri Matisse The Snail, 1953

Vincent Van Gogh
Sunflowers, 1887-1889

Yayoi Kusama
Pumpkin,
(yellow),
Pumpkin
(red),
2016